The First Thing My Mama Told Me

SUSAN MARIE SWANSON

Illustrated by

CHRISTINE DAVENIER

HARCOURT, INC.

San Diego   New York   London

www.harcourt.com

Library of Congress Cataloging-in-Publication Data
Swanson, Susan Marie.
The first thing my mama told me/Susan Marie Swanson; illustrated by
Christine Davenier.
p. cm.
Summary: A young girl celebrates the name that was chosen just
for her.
[1. Names, Personal—Fiction.   2. Identity—Fiction.]
I. Davenier, Christine, ill.   II. Title.
PZ7.S97255Fi   2002
[E]—dc21   2001000986
ISBN 0-15-201075-0

First edition
H G F E D C B A

Manufactured in China

The illustrations in this book were done in pencil, inks, and pastel.
The display type was set in Big Dog.
The text type was set in Electra.
Color separations by Bright Arts Graphics Pte. Ltd., Singapore
Manufactured by South China Printing Company, Ltd., China
This book was printed on totally chlorine-free Nymolla Matte Art paper.
Production supervision by Sandra Grebenar and Pascha Gerlinger
Designed by Ivan Holmes

For my mother and father, with love
—S. M. S.

When I was born,
the first thing my mama told me
was my name.

Mama says she told everyone
who I was,
and she wrote my name
everywhere.
She wrote my name
in my Mother Goose book.
She wrote it
on the backs of pictures,
like the picture of me sleeping
crooked in my car seat,
and the one of me chewing
my pom-pom cap.

Mama says my name comes
from a long-ago word
for light.
When I was born,
she let that name shine on me.

When I was one,
my grandpa spread frosting
on the birthday cupcakes.
Then he squeezed yellow letters
out of a tube.
He kept squeezing
until my whole name appeared.

Mama took a picture of me
smooshing my chocolate cupcake
and my yellow name.
Grandpa says
when I picked that cupcake up,
it looked like a rocket taking off.
My name was the fire
whooshing out.

$\mathcal{W}$hen I was two,
   Uncle David made a step stool for me.
   He cut wood with his electric saw,
   nailed the pieces together,
   and sanded the edges smooth.
   He painted my name on top,
   then painted chipmunks
   running around my name.
   He painted trees
   so the chipmunks and my name
   would have some shade.

When I got thirsty,
I stood on my name
to get a cup of water
all by myself.

When I was three,
I scribbled my name
everywhere.

I rubbed my name
with my finger
on the steamy window.
I zigzagged my name
with chalk
on the front steps.
I colored it
on my hand
with a green marker.
I squiggled it
on the floor
with an orange crayon.
I splashed my name
on the table
with red paint.

I thought everything
belonged to me.
My scribbles said so.

When I was four,
my dad made alphabet pancakes.
He flipped my name onto my plate,
one letter at a time.
I ate the L with maple syrup.
I ate the U with jam.
I ate the C with apple butter.
I ate the Y all by itself.

My name tasted wonderful.

Also when I was four,
I got a baby sister
named Madeline.
She could not eat
her big long name,
so I helped.

When I was five,
I found my name on a coat hook
at kindergarten.
I hung up my sweater
right under my name.

One day I lost my sweater
on the playground.
I looked under the slide
and by the swings.
I couldn't find it anywhere.

The next day, I looked
in the lost and found.
In the jumble of mittens and jackets
and caps,
there were two crumpled sweaters
just the same,
but one had my name
in Mama's tiny writing
on the tag.
I hung my sweater back up
in its own place,
under my name,
where it belonged.

When I was six,
I stomped my name in the snow.
The snow was my paper.
The letters I made
were bigger than me.
My name was part of the hill,
big enough for the sun
and moon to read.

After supper
I wrote a letter to Uncle David
to tell him
about the snow paper
and my giant name.
I told him
how I would not let Madeline
write over my name
with her boots.
I signed my name
at the end of the letter.
Madeline signed hers, too.

Today I am seven.
When Dad lit the candles
on my birthday cake,
Madeline said they looked like stars.

We ate our cake in the backyard,
under the stars in the sky.

Then I opened birthday presents.
I got a poster of the planets
that Grandpa sent,
and a puzzle Madeline helped pick out.
Uncle David sent a book
with empty pages,
and a packet of pencils
with one word stamped on them:
LUCY—
my golden name.

After Dad and Madeline went inside
to wrap up the leftover cake,
Mama told me to hold out my hands
and close my eyes.

Her surprise for me was
a flashlight of my very own.
I clicked it on.
I swirled that new flashlight,
to write my name on the dark.
The letters lit up bricks and grass,
path and swing,
and willow leaves whispering
in the breeze.

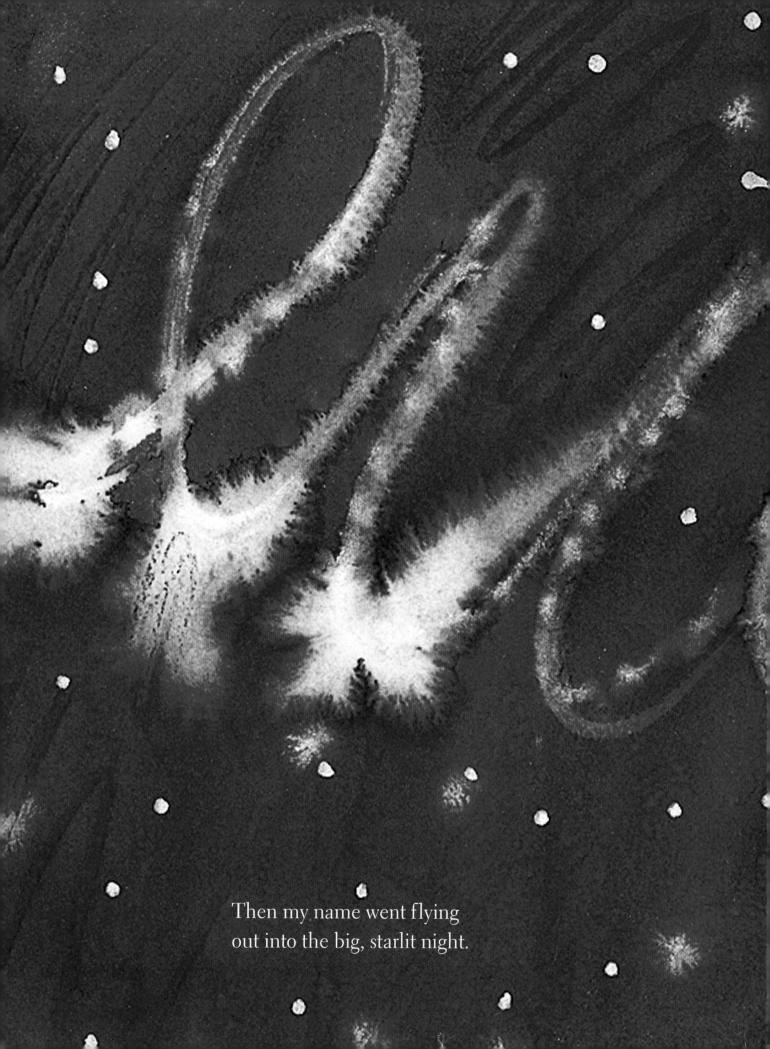

Then my name went flying
out into the big, starlit night.

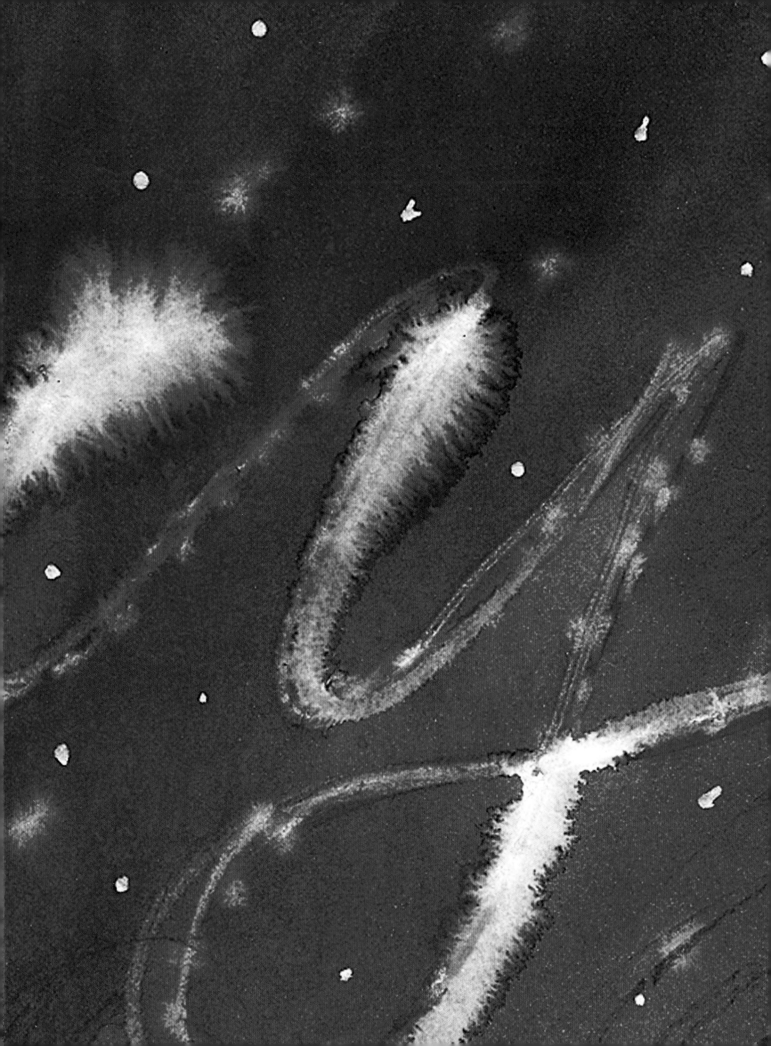

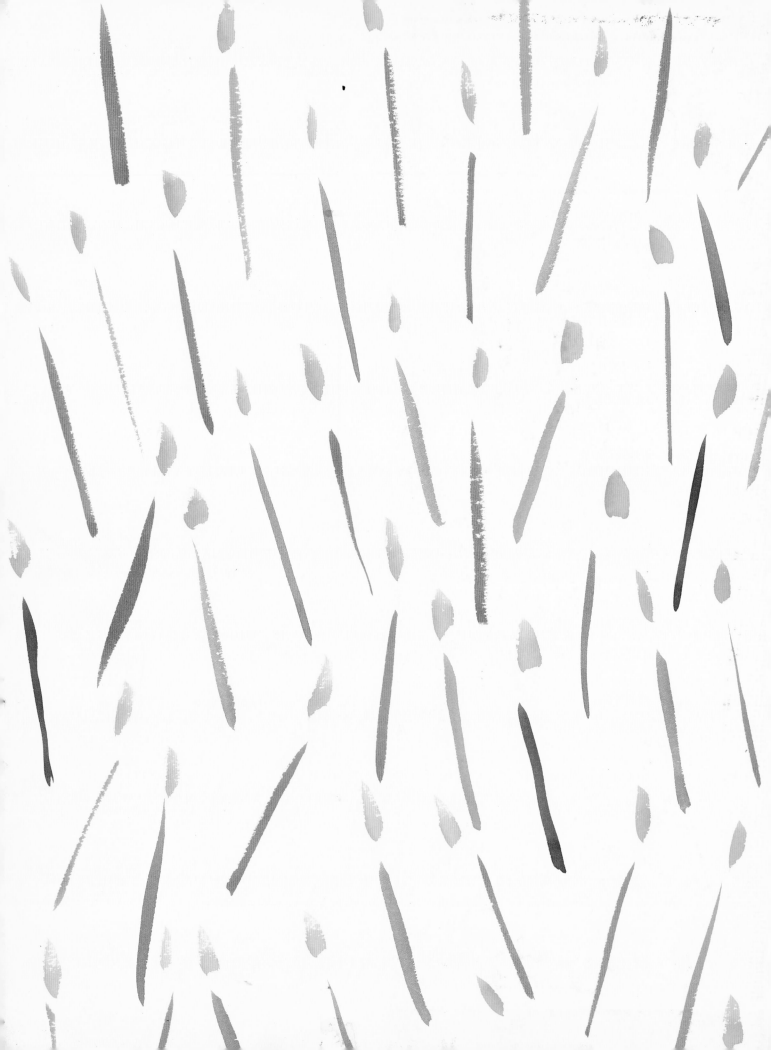